HENRIETTA KING

RANCHER AND PHILANTHROPIST

HENRIETTA KING
RANCHER AND PHILANTHROPIST

Judy Alter

Illustrated by Patrick Messersmith

State House Press

McMurry University

Abilene, Texas

Library of Congress Cataloging-in-Publication Data

Alter, Judy, 1938-
    Henrietta King: rancher and philanthropist / Judy Alter;
    illustrated by Patrick Messersmith.
        p. cm.–(Stars of Texas series)
    Includes bibliographical references and index.
    ISBN-13: 978-1-880510-98-8 (hardcover: alk. paper)
    ISBN-10: 1-880510-98-7 (hardcover: alk. paper)
    1. King, Henrietta Chamberlain, 1832-1925–Juvenile literature. 2.Ranchers–Texas–
Biography–Juvenile literature. 3. Women ranchers–Texas–Biography–Juvenile
literature. 4. King Ranch (Tex.)–Juvenile literature. 5. Philanthropists–Texas–
Biography–Juvenile literature. 6. Women philanthropists–Texas–Biography–Juvenile
literature. 7. Texas–Biography–Juvenile literature. I. Messersmith, Patrick, ill.
II. Title. III. Series.

F392.K47A45 2005
976.4'47063'092–dc22
[B]

2005017298

State House Press
McMurry Station, Box 637
Abilene, TX 79697-0637

Distributed by the Texas A&M University Press Consortium
(800) 826-8911 • www.tamu.edu/upress

Printed in the United States of America

ISBN 1-880510-98-7

Book designed by Rosenbohm Graphic Design

THE STARS OF TEXAS SERIES

Other books in this series include:

Mirabeau B. Lamar: Second President of Texas

CONTENTS

Chapter 1

INTRODUCTION

✳✳✳✳✳

Few women have run the largest ranch in the United States, raised a family, built a city and a railroad, and survived raids by hostile soldiers and Mexican bandits. Henrietta King did all that. The ranch is the famous King Ranch in South Texas.

Henrietta King lived two lives. She was the daughter of a Presbyterian minister. Her mother died when she was very young and her father sent her to an eastern girls school, where she learned fine manners and foreign languages. He expected her to marry a minister and lead a quiet life. Instead, she married an uneducated boat captain and South Texas rancher. She spent her life on barren land in South Texas.

Henrietta King was inducted into the National Cowgirl Hall of Fame in 1982.

✳✳✳

RANCH WIFE

During the early years of the ranch, Henrietta's life was difficult. She and her children lived in a jacal, a hut made of sticks and plastered over with mud. The ranch grew and was successful, and Richard King moved his family into a large house. He and Henrietta had five children. She cared for her children and cooked meals. Like any ranch wife, she worked hard.

Henrietta King also took care of the Mexicans who lived on the ranch and worked there. She made sure their children were educated. She learned their folkways, including those of the *curandera*. She knew to use garlic to take the fire out of a wasp sting or to cure ringworm.

The King Ranch today is an international business and is still owned by Henrietta King's descendants.

During the Civil War, Richard King had to flee his home. Henrietta stayed at the ranch, even when Union soldiers invaded it. Richard King died in 1885, leaving Henrietta in charge of the ranch. The ranch house burned in 1912. During the 1916 Mexican Revolution bandits attacked the ranch several times. Henrietta saw the ranch through all these disasters.

Whether she was in a mud jacal or a grand house, Henrietta King brought civilization and culture to the King Ranch. She did not allow drinking or cursing by any of the men on the ranch. This included the vaqueros who worked for her husband. She also did not allow dancing, except once a year to celebrate Christmas. She always wore a proper dress. When out in the sun, she protected her face with a bonnet.

Mrs. King entertained some of the United States' most famous people of her day. She was equally at home in the parlor and in the pasture. She entertained at the ranch as graciously as if she were in a grand house in a big city.

※※※

Widow and Businessperson

After her husband died, Henrietta King wore the black mourning dress of a widow for forty years. She managed the ranch with her son-in-law, Robert Kleberg, and they built it into an empire. Henrietta King was a very good businesswoman. When she died, she left her children and grandchildren a ranch of nearly a million acres of land and 95,000 head of cattle.

Henrietta King was also a philanthropist. She gave the land for the city of Kingsville, Texas, which sits in the middle of the King Ranch. She had the First Presbyterian Church in Kingsville built and donated land for the Baptist, Methodist, Episcopal, and Catholic churches in that city. She gave money to the town for a public high school. She donated land for a Texas-Mexican Industrial Institute, a hospital, and South Texas State Teachers College (now Texas A&M University-Kingsville).

A philanthropist is a person who donates a lot of money to good causes.

✳✳✳

HENRIETTA'S LEGACY

Today the King Ranch is the largest ranch in the United States. The original Santa Gertrudis Ranch is one of four divisions within the larger King Ranch. Henrietta's descendants still manage and control the ranch. Henrietta King, raised to be ladylike, lived an adventurous life and helped build an empire. Her legend lives on through the King Ranch and her descendants.

Chapter Two

From Missouri
to a Texas Ranch

✳✳✳✳✳

Henrietta Chamberlain was born in Boonville, Missouri, in 1832. Her father, Hiram, was a Presbyterian minister. He and Henrietta's mother, Maria, were missionaries who preached in St. Louis and several small towns in Missouri. When Henrietta was three, her mother died. Her father remarried, but his second wife also died, and Hiram married for a third time. Henrietta had three younger brothers, born to the third marriage of her father. When she was young, her family moved frequently from place to place. Henrietta was always close to her father, but her childhood was lonely, and she learned to be independent.

Henrietta's father's many letters were collected in a book titled, My Dear Henrietta. *This book tells about Henrietta's life from 1846 until 1866, as seen through her father's eyes. The book is now out of print but can occasionally be found in rare book collections.*

Hiram Chamberlain moved his family from Missouri to Tennessee. In 1846 he sent fourteen-year-old Henrietta to the Holly Springs Female Institute in Tennessee, a finishing school. She studied grammar, algebra, moral philosophy, French, and practical household skills like needlework. While she was at school, her father wrote her long letters of advice. He told her to sit up straight to avoid consumption (tuberculosis) and diphtheria (an infection that makes it difficult to breath). He cautioned her to learn to spell. When she wrote that she was homesick, he told her, "We were not made to be perfectly happy here." Hiram Chamberlain could be a stern man. Henrietta finished school in 1848.

Richard King was an orphan and a runaway. He had little education. He was a boat captain.

✳✳✳

THE MOVE TO TEXAS

In 1849 Hiram Chamberlain moved his family to Brownsville, Texas. The city needed a preacher. Henrietta was seventeen. She traveled with her father, her stepmother, and her half-brothers.

One story is that they arrived in Brownsville by boat. Henrietta's stepmother complained a great deal about the difficult trip. Reverend Chamberlain had to take care of Henrietta's baby brother. The family story, however, is that they arrived by stagecoach. Mr. Chamberlain rode horseback next to the coach.

In Brownsville they rented a houseboat named the *Whiteville*. That's how Henrietta met Richard King.

✳✳✳

RICHARD KING

Richard King was born in New York City in 1824. His parents died when he was five, and an aunt raised him. At the age of nine, he was apprenticed to a jeweler. He had to sweep, run errands, and take orders. When he was eleven, he stowed away on a schooner bound for the Gulf of Mexico. The captain of the boat discovered him but didn't throw him off. Instead he made Richard his cabin boy. For the next several years he learned how to pilot steamboats up and down rivers.

In Texas as a young man, King went into partnership with Mifflin Kenedy. Their shipping company was M. Kenedy and Co. They had a contract to supply forts along the Rio Grande River.

Henrietta's father's gift to the newlyweds was a Bible. On the flyleaf he had written, "Read, Believe, Obey, Live."

✳✳✳

A DIFFICULT FIRST MEETING

In February 1850 King piloted his ship into the harbor at Brownsville. He was hot, tired, and dirty from hard work. Another boat was docked in the space reserved for his boat. King began to yell and curse the owner of the other boat. Henrietta Chamberlain appeared on the deck of the *Whiteville*. It was a dilapidated houseboat the Chamberlains were renting because no other quarters were available in the small, new city.

Henrietta was a proper young lady of the 1850s. She wore the long skirts and sleeves and high neck-dress of the day. Her hair was parted in the middle and pulled into a bun at the back of her neck. She stood straight and tall.

Richard King called the *Whiteville* a filthy rat-trap. In perfect English, Henrietta scolded him for indecent language unfit for decent ears. Legend has it that King fell in love immediately but that Henrietta did not much like this rough man.

Later King and Mifflin Kenedy were walking in Brownsville and they met Henrietta. Since Kenedy had met her before, he properly introduced Richard King to her.

✳✳✳

CHURCHES AND SCHOOLS

Hiram Chamberlain held his first church service on the *Whiteville* in February 1850, but his services were not well attended. The people of Brownsville found his sermons dull, so only his family and a few other people came to hear him preach.

Henrietta wanted to establish a school and talked to the parents of the few Anglo children in the area. She believed that education was as important for girls as for boys and that they should go to school together. The parents were horrified because co-ed education was unheard of at that time. So, she opened a girls' school. Henrietta began to learn Spanish and learn about Mexico, and she passed out Bibles and pamphlets about the Presbyterian Church to Mexican citizens. They were almost all members of the Roman Catholic Church.

✳✳✳

Courtship and Marriage

Henrietta Chamberlain was engaged to Charles Stansbury of Brownsville, an educated young man and a Sunday school superintendent. In 1851, Henrietta broke off the engagement. No one knows the reason.

Meanwhile, Richard King began to attend Reverend Chamberlain's church services. He was not a churchgoer, but he wanted to see Henrietta. They probably attended dances in nearby Matamoros, Mexico. They would not have attended together, however. They would have met at public holidays such as the Fourth of July or perhaps at small parties in private homes. Public excursions to battlefields of the recent Mexican-American War were popular. King and Henrietta may have gone on such excursions.

Richard began to court her. Richard and Henrietta often walked together through Brownsville, but King was careful not to walk the preacher's daughter past any saloons. He found that he could talk to her about his dreams for the future, his business, and his difficult childhood.

Richard King was gone from Brownsville for long periods of time. He had to be away on the river, overseeing his shipping business. He also spent a great deal of time on his ranch. Henrietta missed him when he was gone. Their courtship lasted three long years.

Henrietta's father did not approve of the courtship. King had little education and no one knew anything about his family. He had once owned a saloon and he liked to drink and fight. He seemed to have no money and no future. Henrietta had always been a devout and obedient daughter, but Reverend Chamberlain had raised her to be independent and to make her own decisions. When she heard that Richard had asked her father for her hand in marriage, Henrietta told her father she would marry Richard. She didn't wait for her father's approval. As King's fortunes improved, Reverend Chamberlain softened his attitude. He admired a good businessman.

Reverend Chamberlain performed the wedding after regular services on Sunday, December 10, 1854. Henrietta was twenty-two years old. She stepped down from the choir loft, where she had been singing. Her wedding gown was peach silk. King stepped up from the first row, where he had been sitting with Mifflin Kenedy and his wife.

Chapter Three

A BRUSH COUNTRY RANCH

✳✳✳✳✳

The South Texas brush country that lies between the Rio Grande and Nueces rivers fascinated King. Once, he and some friends rode north from Brownsville to Corpus Christi. The land was so barren that they did not see water for over a hundred miles. Richard King purchased some land in this area in 1853.

The brush country was land where prickly things grow best—mesquite, cactus, chaparral, and catclaw. Sometimes the uncleared brush was too thick to ride a horse through. In the 1850s herds of wild horses roamed the land, which became known as Wild Horse Desert. Deer, antelope, wild turkey, quail, rattlesnakes, and buzzards also lived there. But there were no ranchers. The only people were mustangers, a few Indians (from the Karankawa tribe and the Lipan Apache family), and outlaws.

Mexican citizens owned title to the land under grants either from the Spanish crown or the Mexican government. They called it the Desert of the Dead, because it had so little water. Most of the water that could be found was undrinkable salt water. The Mexicans had abandoned the land. The United States flag flew over it since the Mexican-American War of 1846-1848, and Mexicans were afraid to live there.

The first water King came to was the Santa Gertrudis Creek, not far from Corpus Christi. Here the land was black loam flatland, and the grass reached to his stirrups. He decided to buy the land. With a partner, Gideon K. "Legs" Lewis, King bought 15,500 acres of land

Richard King took his bride to his Santa Gertrudis ranch on their honeymoon. They lived in a jacal.

for $300 from a land grant known as Rincón de Santa Gertrudis. Later Legs Lewis was killed, and King became the only owner of the ranch.

At first the ranch was just a cow camp with mesquite corrals, but King continued to buy land. He looked for land with water on it, and he raised cattle to sell for hides and tallow. He traveled to Mexico to buy horses and cattle.

In the town of Cruillas he bought all the horses and longhorn cattle available. The people had no way left to make a living, so he invited them to live on his Santa Gertrudis land and work for wages. The entire town moved with him—one hundred men, women, and children. They all made the trip to the ranch together in one big procession called the "entrada" or entrance. The new

Texas Rangers helped protect frontier homesteads from Indian and bandit raids. The Texas Rangers are still in existence today.

residents became known as Los Kineños, "the King People," and they were very loyal to Richard King. They called him "El Capitán." The men were vaqueros who were wise about cattle because their ancestors had raised cattle on the land for centuries. Many of their sons and grandsons followed their example as vaqueros on the King Ranch.

Because of the threat of Indian raids and bandits, the ranch had to be protected at all times. A company of Texas Rangers patrolled the Corpus Christi area and kept the ranch safe.

✳✳✳

A Ranch Honeymoon

For their honeymoon, Richard King brought Henrietta to his ranch, 120 miles from Brownsville. They traveled in a stagecoach for four days. Armed guards rode beside the stagecoach and stood guard over the camps at night. A cook from the ranch prepared campfire meals.

Back in Henrietta's time, most women rode horses using a sidesaddle, designed so that a woman's full skirts completely covered her legs.

Henrietta thought the land did not look at all like what Richard had described to her. There was a bad drought in 1854, and the grass had shriveled and died. Water holes had dried up. She didn't realize that the land would be green again when another year brought rain.

The ranch Henrietta first saw had a few jacals, some mesquite corrals, a commissary, and a blockhouse and stockade with a cannon. Protection and safety came first.

Henrietta and Richard lived in a jacal. The pantry was so small that Henrietta hung her large platters on the outside walls. She entertained an occasional traveler and everyone had to dress for dinner, even in the jacal. "Dressing for dinner" involved brushing the travel dust off clothes and washing hands and faces.

Ranching in the 1850s meant owning large branded herds of unfenced and half-wild cattle. Richard rode all over the ranch to check his livestock. When he rode within a day of the ranch, Henrietta rode with him. She made herself a divided skirt so she could ride astride and keep up with him. She had never ridden anything but a sidesaddle before.

Richard's first cattle brand was HK—for Henrietta King. Later he registered the Running W, still used by the ranch today.

Henrietta entered into the life of the ranch, looking after the welfare of the Kineños. She nursed the sick, helped the needy, and educated their children. The vaqueros learned that she did not allow cursing and that they had to hide their whiskey and mescal (liquor made from cactus).

The Kings were careful to help the Kineños keep their Roman Catholic religion and their Mexican customs. They ate traditional foods and sang traditional songs. Henrietta King once said, "The King Ranch started with Spanish people and the King Ranch will end with Spanish people."

The Kineños called her "La Patrona," meaning patron, defender, saint, protector, master, employer, or boss. All their married life, Henrietta called her husband "The Captain." He called her "Etta."

The King family kept a home in Brownsville, but Henrietta always wanted to live on the ranch.

✳✳✳

A HOME IN BROWNSVILLE

Richard frequently had to leave the ranch to take care of business in Brownsville, but he didn't like leaving Henrietta behind. He decided they should have two houses—one at the ranch and one in Brownsville. Henrietta planned the cottage that they built on Elizabeth Street in Brownsville, next door to Mifflin Kenedy and his wife.

Colonel Robert E. Lee of the United States Army was a frequent visitor in Brownsville and at the ranch between 1856 and 1861. (He would later be commanding general of the Confederate army.) He and King met on a steamship and became immediate friends, and Henrietta also liked and admired Lee. The story is that he picked out the site on high ground where the ranch's permanent home was built.

Richard would not allow Henrietta to stay at the ranch when she was expecting their first child, so he moved her to Brownsville until after the baby was born. He stopped traveling so he could be with her when the baby arrived. Henrietta Maria, called Nettie, was born April 17, 1856. Her grandfather baptized her.

Henrietta wrote late in life that her favorite food was venison.

To care for the people of the ranch, Henrietta King learned the ways of the curanderas, Mexican healing women believed to have magical, spiritual healing powers.

Henrietta did not like being left behind in Brownsville when Richard went to the ranch. By the time Nettie was six months old, she was traveling to the ranch with her parents. Once when they were camped for the night, a Mexican asked to join their camp. Richard sent him for firewood. Henrietta looked up just in time to call out. The Mexican was approaching Richard with a knife drawn. Richard threw him to the ground and then banished him from the camp.

Another time Henrietta was alone in the jacal with Nettie. She had been baking bread and had several fresh loaves laid out. An Indian suddenly stood in the doorway. He jumped toward the cradle and waved a club, threatening to attack the baby. Then he pointed to the bread. Henrietta gave it all to him.

Richard King posted a guard at the family house at all times. He wanted Henrietta to move to Brownsville, but she wanted to stay on the ranch.

Ella Morse King was born in April 1858 in Brownsville. Henrietta brought the baby back to the ranch almost immediately after her birth.

***

TROUBLE WITH BANDITS

In spite of the Kineños, not all Mexican citizens were friendly to American settlers. Many thought their land had been stolen from them. A Mexican outlaw named Juan Cortina hated Americans.

In 1859, Richard King took his family on a summer trip to Kentucky to buy thoroughbred horses for the ranch's breeding program. Henrietta's half-brother, Hiram, Jr., went with them and stayed in Kentucky to attend college.

In one of his business ventures, Richard King designed special boats that would navigate the narrow bends and fast currents of the Rio Grande River.

While the Kings were in Kentucky, Cortina captured Brownsville. He and about forty men rode through town shouting, "Death to Americans." They set fire to many buildings. A Mexican general, José Carbajal, persuaded Cortina to leave Brownsville, but trouble continued. Cortina eventually raised an army of several hundred men. U.S. Army troops under General Robert E. Lee defeated him.

The King Ranch was not touched during the so-called Cortina Wars, but many of its cattle were driven across the border. Captain King was more worried than ever about his family.

✳✳✳

A Move to the Ranch House

Richard King knew the Civil War was coming, and he also knew he and Mifflin Kenedy would need more boats. He spent much of his time in Brownsville, preparing for his part in the war.

In December 1860 Henrietta was expecting a child any moment. She decided she could not wait at the ranch any longer and set out for town in a stagecoach. Richard King, Jr., was born on December 15 in the stage-coach.

Henrietta was not content in Brownsville. She wanted her children to grow up on the ranch and she insisted on moving the family back there.

In 1858 the first permanent ranch house was built at the Santa Gertrudis. The "Big House" was a one-and-a-half-story frame house with an attic and a large veran-dah. The dining room and kitchen were in separate buildings made of stone to avoid fire. A men's dormitory

Robert E. Lee was a frequent visitor to the ranch. He later became commanding general of the Confederacy during the Civil War.

was built for buyers, visitors, and occasional travelers. By then the ranch had a commissary with a kitchen and dining area, stables, corrals, wagon sheds, and houses for the Kineños. With Henrietta's urging, Richard built a schoolhouse in the 1860s.

Chapter Four

THE CIVIL WAR

✳✳✳✳✳

Richard King was a loyal Southerner during the Civil War. King and Kenedy registered their new boats in Mexico so the Union army could not seize the boats. Union ships blockaded southern ports so no cotton could be shipped to Europe and sold. The Confederacy needed to sell the cotton for money to fight the war. King and Kenedy shipped cotton from Mexican ports to British ships waiting in the Gulf of Mexico. The cotton was carried in wagons across the King Ranch to Mexico.

The ranch was also a collection point for Confederate cattle to be shipped to England. The commissary at the ranch sold supplies, mules, and beef to the wagon masters who transported cotton for

During the Civil War, cotton was the most valuable crop for southern states because it could be exchanged in Europe for much needed ammunition, medicines, and weapons.

shipment to England. Richard King was clearly an enemy of the Union.

Alice Gertrudis King was born April 29, 1862. She was the first King child to be born on the ranch. Henrietta tried to keep daily life normal for the children, but there were Union raiding parties in the border area. King had to raise his own army to protect his family, his cattle, and his land. His soldiers were Kineños.

In 1863 a unit of Texas Confederate soldiers camped at the ranch. The Kineños would not let them camp near the house. Instead, Richard King rode to their camp and when he saw that they were disciplined, he fed them. His first concern was always for his family. After that it was for his people and the South's cotton.

In 1864 Union ships anchored at the mouth of the Rio Grande River in Brownsville, causing the town's citizens to flee. Hiram Chamberlain and his sons rode to the ranch.

Union soldiers first invaded the town of Brownsville in November 1863 and then reoccupied the town on July 30, 1864.

The Union troops dumped residents' rifles in the river and burned all the cotton they could find. They stole things from people's houses and vandalized property. Much of the town was destroyed.

✳✳✳

AN ATTACK ON THE RANCH

Union officers knew the King Ranch was an important stop on the Confederate cattle and cotton route. In December 1864 King was warned that the Yankees would attack the ranch at any moment. He had to flee, but he didn't want to leave Henrietta and the children. She assured him they would be fine. Soldiers would not touch children and a woman who was expecting her fifth child.

King asked Francisco Alvarado, a loyal Kineño, to guard his family. Henrietta organized supplies for the ranch house and prepared for an attack.

The Union soldiers arrived at dawn on Christmas Eve. They fired rifles at the house and Henrietta ordered everyone to get down on the floor. Then the soldiers shouted that they would set fire to the house. Francisco Alvarado rushed out the door to tell them there were women and children inside. The soldiers shot and killed him because they thought he was Richard King.

The soldiers invaded the house. They rode their horses inside and slashed the draperies with swords. They took clothing and smashed windows, mirrors, and china. The Union soldiers took horses and mules and made prisoners of some of the men at the ranch. A

Barbed wire changed life in the American West. It was cheap and easy to install. It brought an end to the days of open cattle ranges and cattle drives north to railroads.

group of Kineños and a band of Texas Rangers finally forced the Union soldiers to leave.

Henrietta knew that it was time for her to take the children away. She took her family to friends in San Patricio, northwest of Corpus Christi, by coach. The driver and relief driver each had shotguns and revolvers, and four armed Kineños rode with them.

Henrietta's fifth and last child, Robert E. Lee King, was born in San Patricio.

When Henrietta was again able to travel, she took her family to San Antonio where they rented a house. For a long time they did not know where Captain King was. Finally they heard he was with Richardson's Company of Black Hatted Rebels. James Richardson was the King ranch foreman and his soldiers were Kineños. At his own request, Captain King was a private (the lowest rank) in the company. King spent a year riding with the company, guarding Confederate cotton shipments.

✳✳✳

THE WAR ENDS

When the war ended, Richard King was considered a traitor because he had fought for the Confederacy, and he was not allowed to take the oath of loyalty to the United States. He was paroled but forced to live in Brownsville and forbidden to return to his ranch which had been seized by the U.S. government. King had not seen his family for almost two years. He requested a pardon from President Andrew Johnson and asked that he be able to return to his land. For many months he heard nothing. Then at long last he was given clear title to his lands. His house was returned to him. He was once again a citizen of the United States.

He immediately went to San Antonio to bring his family back to the ranch.

King took presents for all the children and his wife. For Henrietta, he had a pair of diamond earrings. Henrietta was torn. Her early church training had taught her that wearing such expensive jewelry was a sign of vanity. But she knew that Richard wanted her to wear the earrings as a symbol of his love. She solved the problem by having the earrings coated with enamel. This dulled them enough that she was not self-conscious about wearing them. She wore them the rest of her life.

Richard King had to rebuild both his ranch and his freight business. He had to buy back his freighters and repair them. Once the freighters were repaired, he could run his business again.

Drovers, vaqueros, cow-hands, and herdsmen are all different words for cowboys.

The years after the Civil War were the Golden Age of the cattle drives. The Midwest needed beef and Texas had more cattle than ever. Thousands of cattle were driven north along marked trails to railroad stations in Kansas. Then they were shipped to eastern markets. Many of those cattle bore the Running W brand of the King Ranch. Holdups were always a danger. Bandits would wait until the cowboys—or drovers, as they were called on cattle drives—had sold the cattle and had the profits in their pockets. Then they would rob them.

Often King himself went on these drives. He hid the money made from selling the herd in a steel strongbox in his coach. Henrietta worried about him because she knew he could be killed on any trip. When he came home he always had presents for Henrietta and the chil-

The term "Midwest" refers to the states located in the middle of the East and West coasts, most commonly the states of Ohio, Indiana, Illinois, Michigan, Wisconsin, Minnesota, Iowa, Missouri, Kansas, and Nebraska.

dren. She was afraid he was spoiling the children. She wanted to teach them thrift, but Richard King did not know the meaning of the word.

King was losing cattle to rustlers who would raid and steal cattle to sell for their own profit. The Texas Rangers could no longer protect the ranch, so King began to fence his range. He didn't use barbed wire like other ranchers because he was afraid it would hurt the cattle. Instead he fenced with mesquite posts laced together with wet rawhide that tightened as it dried. Even with the fences, rustlers drove many of his cattle to Mexico.

Richard King and Mifflin Kenedy brought a lawsuit to stop trespassing on a road that ran across both their ranches. The opposing lawyer was a young, new lawyer from Corpus Christi named Robert Justus Kleberg. Kleberg won the case, and Richard King was so impressed that he hired him to clear titles to King land. The titles to many parcels of land were in confusion after the Mexican-American War of 1846-1848 and after the Civil War.

✳✳✳

THE CHILDREN GROW UP

Henrietta paid close attention to the upbringing of her children. She was concerned about their schooling and their experiences. She thought that children should travel, so she took three-year-old Robert E. Lee King to see General Lee in Virginia. They talked about the size of herds and the purchase of Shorthorn and Kentucky Durham cattle. The children were sent to boarding schools. Nettie went to a Presbyterian girls' school in St. Louis. Ella and Alice went to a seminary in St. Louis.

Soon after completing her schooling, Nettie married in St. Louis. Ella married at the ranch. The

Richard and Henrietta King had three daughters and two sons—Henrietta Marie, Ella, Richard Jr., Alice, and Lee.

Today 570 styles of barbed wire are patented. Many people collect samples of the different styles as a hobby.

boys were away at school. Richard had sent young Richard to college in Kentucky with his own man-servant and carriage. Without children, Henrietta found the ranch lonesome. She visited all of them often. When grandchildren came, her visits were even more frequent.

Word came to the ranch that Lee, as Robert E. Lee King was called, was ill with pneumonia at his school in St. Louis. Richard and Henrietta rushed to their son's side. On March 1, 1883, he died, with his parents at his bedside. Both parents were heartbroken. Lee had loved the land, and Richard had been counting on him to take over the ranch.

Henrietta avoided the ranch that Lee had loved. She couldn't bear the memories. But when she heard that Richard had decided to sell their land, she went home. "Never sell," she told him, repeating his old lessons to her. "Buy land."

***

RICHARD KING DIES

Richard's health had been failing for some time. He had stomach pains and could not eat. He knew that something serious was wrong with him. He had planned to turn the ranch over to Lee as soon as possible, but now he didn't know who would take control of the land and the operations.

Richard, Jr., married and was given forty thousand acres and a house near the main ranch. His ranch was called Rancho Puerta de Agua Dulce, and he planned to raise oranges and cotton. His father didn't believe in turning rangeland into farmland, but he was too sick to raise an argument.

Henrietta took Richard, Sr., to San Antonio to see a specialist. The doctor confirmed what Richard suspected. He was in the final stages of cancer of the stomach. He died on April 14, 1885, in the Menger Hotel at San Antonio. He was sixty-two. Henrietta was fifty-three. She had lost her father, a brother, one of her sons, and now her husband within a few years.

Chapter Five

INTO THE TWENTIETH CENTURY

✳✳✳✳✳

Captain King left everything to his wife. He had confidence she would do things exactly as he would have. She was the only owner of the large ranch for more than forty years.

Henrietta inherited a half million acres of land and $1.5 million dollars in debt. She turned over the daily running of the ranch to Robert Kleberg, the lawyer Richard had hired several years before. Kleberg had been learning about the ranch for several years. He had learned to ride horseback and to speak Spanish. The Kineños called him "El Abrogado," Spanish for "the lawyer." He consulted Henrietta on all major decisions.

In 1888 Henrietta's step-brother, Willie Chamberlain, was bitten by a rabid coyote. The family physician, Dr. Arthur Spahn, took him to France for a new vaccine. It saved his life.

Henrietta began to pay off debts. She decided to send fewer cattle to market because the cattle market was down and prices were low. She would keep the cattle for breeding. Other ranchers always wanted King Ranch cattle for stock. Land prices were also low, so Henrietta used the cash she got from selling breeding stock to buy more land. By the late 1890s, she owned a million acres.

Henrietta's decisions made ranching history. A new breed of cattle was developed. Cattle were dipped in vats to prevent ticks. She proved that artesian wells could bring water to South Texas.

In June 1886, Henrietta's daughter, Alice King, married Robert Kleberg in a quiet ceremony at the ranch. They took Henrietta on their honeymoon because they

The King Ranch developed a new breed of cattle called the Santa Gertrudis, which is a mix between Shorthorn and Brahman cattle.

didn't want her to be left alone at the ranch. When they returned, Alice took over running the house.

It was a busy household. By 1898 Alice and Robert had five children. Business guests and friends often joined the family, and the same rules still applied to all: no hard liquor and fresh clothes for dinner. At dinnertime Henrietta led a procession from the main house to the dining building, and she sat at the head of the table.

The Big House was enlarged for the third time. A two-story, ten-bedroom addition was built on the back of the house, and galleries or open porches extended the length of both floors. More trees were planted. The driveway was paved with crushed shells. Around 1900, telephones and electricity were brought to the house as well as hot and cold running water.

By the 1890s, Henrietta saw two big problems facing the ranch: drought and transportation. Cattle were dying for lack of water, and Henrietta had the Kineños skin them so the hides could be sold. She ordered wells dug until water was found, no matter how deep. It was 1899 before drillers found an artesian spring. She ordered the men to drill in other places. The ranch needed to grow grass on as much land as possible for the cattle to eat.

✳✳✳

A Railroad and a City

The ranch needed a way to get its cattle to market. The days of the cattle drives were over. Ranges were fenced, and cattle could no longer easily pass from one range to another on their way north. Henrietta saw a railroad as the solution, so several prominent citizens and old friends of King went together to build the St. Louis, Brownsville & Mexico Railroad. It ran from Corpus Christi to Brownsville and

The King Ranch is located in four different counties-- Nueces, Kenedy, Kleberg, and Willacy.

back. Henrietta donated land for the right of way so the train could cross ranch property. The train made its first run on January 4, 1904. Cannons boomed, flags flew, and a band blared to celebrate the occasion.

The train took nine hours to go from Corpus Christi to Brownsville. A stagecoach took forty hours. But the train did not run on Sundays. Henrietta's school-age grandchildren always took the train from Corpus Christi on Fridays.

Henrietta donated 853 acres in the middle of the ranch for the city of Kingsville. It was laid out in 266 city blocks, and some of the streets were named King, Kenedy, Henrietta, and Santa Gertrudis. Other streets were named for her children. Henrietta did not allow saloons in Kingsville. By 1905 the city had a population of almost one thousand.

Henrietta operated several businesses in Kingsville—the Kingsville Lumber Company, the Kingsville Publishing Company that produced a weekly newspaper, the Gulf Coast Cotton Gin Company, and the Kleberg Town & Improvement Company. She and Robert Kleberg also built an icehouse to help farmers ship their produce to market before it spoiled. Henrietta had the first public school in Kingsville built in 1906. It had one teacher and thirteen students. Later she donated land and $75,000 for a twenty-two-room school.

A Tragic Fire

In April 1912 the "Big House" caught fire during the night. It was, as always, full of family and guests, and all got out safely. Henrietta put her jewelry in one bag

The King Ranch is larger than the state of Rhode Island.

Henrietta King and her son-in-law, Robert Justus Kleberg, built the ranch into the largest ranch in the United States.

and her medications in another and walked out the front door, dressed in her black dress, carrying her two bags. Robert Kleberg saved some of the records and cash from the safe. Kineños wanted to go in after the grand piano, but Henrietta stopped them because she did not want them to risk their lives.

A new, fireproof house of concrete covered with stucco was built within two years at a cost of $250,000. Each of its twenty-five rooms had its own fireplace. The dining hall seated fifty. The house had the security of a fortress, peacocks on the front lawn, and a patio with tropical trees and shrubs. Henrietta was eighty when her new house was built. She said she wanted a house where anyone could walk in boots, so the floors were mesquite wood and slate. The new house was called "Casa Grande."

✳✳✳

A New Breed of Cattle

The ranch had replaced the original longhorn cattle with English breeds. It now had large herds of Shorthorn and Hereford cattle, which were bred for colder climates, and took sick and died in the Texas heat. A longhorn could survive the heat, but it was a scrawny, tough animal and its meat was not as good.

The King Ranch bred Brahman cattle into the Shorthorn herd. Brahmans were from India, and were used to the hot climate and stayed disease free. But they were mean and hard to handle and they did not produce good beef. When Brahman cattle were bred to Shorthorns, however, they produced hardy cattle that provided good meat. The ranch registered them

The Henrietta King Memorial Center in Kingsville has a large collection of materials relating to Henrietta King's life.

Pancho Villa, a bandit and an outlaw, was a hero of the Mexican Revolution. He was seen by the poor people as a Mexican Robin Hood, taking from the rich to give to the poor. He made frequent raids into the United States and probably raided the King Ranch more than once.

as the Santa Gertrudis breed. The breed traces back to a Brahman bull so ugly that he was named Monkey.

✸✸✸

MORE RAIDS ON THE RANCH

By 1916, Mexico was in the midst of a rebellion. Rebel leaders like Pancho Villa often crossed the border to steal cattle and goods, and several King Ranch cowboys were killed.

The ranch was warned it was about to be raided, so Henrietta directed the organization of defenses. Men armed with rifles, ammunition, and field glasses were stationed on the roof of the house and a searchlight was put in place. When all was done to her satisfaction, Henrietta went to bed.

The raiders saw a small army waiting for them and turned back. There was no trouble at the ranch that night.

In all, during those troubled times, the ranch was raided twenty-six times. Trains crossing the ranch property were derailed and robbed several times.

✳✳✳

THE END OF AN ERA

During World War I, Robert Kleberg's health failed. He turned the ranch over to Robert, Jr., then twenty-one years old. Young Robert wanted to concentrate ranch resources on cattle and did not want to continue selling land to farmers. Henrietta agreed with her grandson because he was following his grandfather's ways. She continued to buy land. She bought a large salt lake to provide the salt the cattle needed and purchased a dry pasture (all sand and no water) because it was near where oil had been discovered. She deeded any interest in petroleum production to the Kleberg branch of the family. With time, it brought them a fortune.

An artesian well is a deep well from which water rises by pressure through a layer of rock between the water and the earth's surface.

Even as her health failed, Henrietta maintained an active interest in the ranch and its cattle. She often joined the roundups, watching from her carriage. At the ranch house, she walked in the gardens and picked vegetables for the day's meals. In her last years nurses walked her each afternoon to her beloved Santa Gertrudis Creek near the house.

Henrietta King died quietly in her sleep at the age of ninety-three on March 31, 1925. She had outlived all of her children except Alice. Her twenty-two-page will, written in 1918, provided for everyone in her family but forbade dissolving the ranch.

Henrietta's funeral was held at the ranch and attended by a great number of friends, her large family, and the ranch's Kineños. Some vaqueros rode two days from distant parts of the ranch to be there.

The funeral procession bore her to Chamberlain Park in Kingsville, the cemetery named for her father. An honor guard of two hundred cowboys escorted the procession. Henrietta was buried next to Captain King, and when the casket was lowered into the grave, the cowboys came forward in single file, each cantering around the open grave once, hat at his side as a salute.

✳✳✳

THE LEGACY

The King Ranch is legendary today as one of the largest privately held corporations in the United States. In the 1930s and 1940s, the ranch had operations in Cuba, Venezuela, Florida,

Argentina, Australia, Spain, and Morocco. At one time it raised prize-winning Thoroughbred racehorses. Today, the ranch has Santa Gertrudis cattle, a few Longhorns for show, quarter horses, and oil and gas wells.

King Ranch headquarters outside Kingsville is a popular tourist attraction, offering daily historical tours. Stores in Kingsville sell souvenir items, from furniture to clothing, with the Running W brand.

The former icehouse is the Henrietta King Memorial Center, named in honor of Henrietta's granddaughter. It houses a museum, a banquet hall, and an archive. The museum has a stagecoach like the one Henrietta rode in on her honeymoon journey to the Santa Gertrudis Ranch.

Timeline

1832—Henrietta Maria Morse Chamberlain is born in Boonville, Missouri

1835—Henrietta's mother dies

1846—Henrietta attends Holly Springs Female Institute in Missouri

1848—She completes her education

1850—Hiram Chamberlain moves his family to Brownsville, Texas; Henrietta, eighteen, meets Richard King; Hiram Chamberlain organizes the first Presbyterian mission in South Texas

1853—Richard King founds the King Ranch on the Santa Gertrudis Creek in the Wild Horse Desert

1854—Henrietta teaches briefly at the Rio Grande Female Institute; she marries Richard King on December 10; they establish their home on the ranch.

1856—Henrietta Marie King is born

1858—Ella Morse King is born

1860—Richard King, Jr., is born

1862—Alice King is born

1863—Richard King leaves the ranch to escape capture by Union forces; Henrietta and the children remain behind.

1864—Robert E. Lee King, called Lee, is born

1883—Robert E. Lee King dies

1885—Richard King dies

1904—Henrietta King donates land for the towns of Kingsville and Raymondville

1912—The "Big House" at the King Ranch burns to the ground

1925—Henrietta King dies at the age of ninety-three; the ranch had increased to 1,173,000 acres

GLOSSARY

Apprentice—an apprentice is a young boy who is legally bound to work for an older person in order to learn a craft or a trade

Artesian well—a deep well from which water rises by pressure through a layer of rock between the water and the earth's surface

Blockade—enemy troops shut a harbor or a port so that ships cannot enter or leave

Commissary—a store that supplies food and equipment, particularly to armies

Curandera—a Mexican woman with the gift of healing

Finishing school—a private high school where young women were taught the social graces to prepare them for life in society. They were not expected to develop a career.

Jacal—a hut made of sticks, plastered over with mud

Missionary—one who is sent by a church into a newly settled area to spread the word of the gospel, usually Christian

Philanthropist—one who donates large amounts of money, property, or time for the good of mankind

Rincón—Spanish for a narrow valley

Siesta—Spanish for a mid-day nap

Thrift—the careful management of money

Vandalize—to deliberately destroy and deface property

Vaquero—a Mexican horseman or herdsman

FURTHER READING

Alter, Judy. *Extraordinary Women of the American West*. Danbury, Connecticut: Childrens Press, 1999.

Crawford, Ann Fears and Crystal Sasse Ragsdale. *Women in Texas*. Abilene, Texas: State House Press, 1992.

Durham, Merle. *The Lone Star State Divided: Texas and the Civil War*. Dallas: Hendrick Long Publishing, 1994.

Fox, Mary Virginia. *A Queen Named King: Henrietta of the King Ranch*. Austin: Eakin Publications, November 1998.

Texas Mothers Committee. *Worthy Mothers of Texas*. Belton, Texas: Stillhouse Hollow, 1976.

WEBSITES

King, Henrietta Chamberlain.
www.tsha.utexas.edu/handbook/online/articles/view/KK/fki16.html

www.king-ranch.com/legend.htm

www.tea.state.tx.us/ssc/teks_and_taas/teks/bio2.htm

www.findagrave.com/cgi-bin/fg.cgi?page=gr&GRid=581&pt=Henrietta%20King

www.factmonster.com/ipka/A0900112.html

INDEX